TRISTIN AND ISOLDE

A Retelling of the Legend

I0456930

Anne Kinsey

TRISTIN AND ISOLDE

A Retelling of the Legend

The stair tower was cold, the air so moist that droplets of water clung to the stone walls. Furious blasts of wind swept through the slits which served as windows, causing the torch mounted along the wall to flicker. The stairs, tightly spiraled, were so steep that Isolde pressed a palm against the wall for balance as she tiptoed down.

She reached the landing. The door to her parent's room was made of heavy wood bolted together with strips of metal. She knew from experience where the boards separated just enough so that, when she pressed her ear to the door, she could hear what her parents were saying. She knelt to listen.

She heard the fire snapping and cracking as someone put on more wood. Then her mother said, "The terms are fair."

"Yes," her father said. "Very fair."

What followed was silence. Isolde waited, shivering again. The silence went on so long she feared they wouldn't say any more even though this was the time they usually discussed important matters. Then her mother said, "Given the things said about the King of Cornwall, perhaps you should just accept his proposal."

"His nephew is here with one dozen armed men ready to do our bidding. Why not have them get rid of the river creature?"

There was a pause followed by rustling sounds. "Why not, indeed?" her mother said.

Footsteps in the room sounded as if they were coming toward the door. Isolde stood up straight, and, as swiftly as she could without making noise or risking a fall, hurried back up the stairs to the next landing.

The wind blew again in a furious gust, this time entirely blowing out the torch overhead, leaving her in darkness. The door to her own room was slightly ajar, showing the light within, so she could feel her way back. Brangwain, her personal maid, was just inside, waiting for her. Seeing Isolde, Brangwain opened the door wider. The hinges creaked loudly.

Once Isolde was safely in the room with the door closed, she said, "That knight, Tristin, brought a proposal from King Mark of Cornwall. My father will send Tristin to kill the river creature."

"I knew it!"

A shudder went through Isolde.

"Here," said Brangwain, picking up a thick quilt. "Put this around your shoulders. Come warm up by the fire."

Isolde and Brangwain sat together on a cushioned bench near the fireplace. Isolde wrapped her skirts around her legs and hugged her knees.

Isolde's bedroom was dominated by a large hooded fireplace, the room sweetened with the scent of herbs mixed with the floor rushes. The room contained a curtained bed draped with burgundy velvet, a bench, a wardrobe, a chest, and three high-backed chairs with tasseled cushions. With the exception of a few tapestries hanging from rods, the gray stone walls were bare. A mirror hung on the wall near the door. High on the opposite wall was a small arched window.

"Do you think Tristin will kill the river creature?" Isolde asked.

"Of course he will!"

The creature that terrorized the villages along the River Slanley was said to be a cross between an extraordinarily large snake and a lizard the size of a man. It was described by some as green with scales, and by others as silvery with skin like chain mail. Some villagers claimed that the creature breathed fire.

Whenever a boat was hurled against the rocks and destroyed, or a farm animal was drowned, the destruction was said to be the work of the river creature. Most recently the creature attacked a child who had waded into the water. The child died from the creature's deadly bite. The local villagers begged Isolde's father to find a way to get rid of the creature.

"Did you see him?" Isolde asked softly.

"Who?" asked Brangwain, startled.

"Tristin!"

"I did. He's King Mark's nephew."

"I saw him, too. He is very handsome."

"You should not be thinking about Tristin," said Brangwain. "You are not going to marry the nephew. You will marry the uncle."

"A man old enough to be my father!"

"He's not as old as that! And he's a *king*, not a mere man, a king praised by everyone who knows him. He's said to be fair, and just, and honest."

Isolde hugged her knees tighter and looked into the fire, which was crackling comfortingly. The flames were low, the logs mostly glowing embers.

"Tristin," Isolde said again, and sighed deeply. She liked the very sound of his name.

"The man you will marry is *Mark*," said Brangwain firmly.

Brangwain and Isolde were almost the same age. Brangwain's family had been in the service of Isolde's father, the King of Leinster, for three generations. Brangwain had been personal maid and companion to Isolde for the past five years. Because Isolde and Brangwain had lived so long in such close proximity, they were more like kinswomen than princess and servant. They even bore faint resemblance. Both had vivid blue eyes and pretty oval-shaped faces, and both were tall and slender, but they were never mistaken for sisters. Even strangers knew at a glance that Isolde, who was always perfectly coifed and groomed, and who moved with grace and confidence and spoke in a voice that was at once musical and lovely and commanding, was of much higher birth.

"But you are betrothed to a handsome man, Brangwain! Why shouldn't I want the same?"

"You have no idea what King Mark looks like. Just because he's thirty-five doesn't mean he can't also be handsome. Besides, I am betrothed to a handsome *blacksmith*. You are a princess, and you will marry a *king*."

This much was true. Unless something went wrong – unless the river creature killed Tristin instead of the other way around, or unless some other mishap occurred before the wedding could be celebrated – she would indeed marry Mark, King of Cornwall.

Next morning just after sunup, a flourish of trumpets came from the courtyard below, and the castle gates clanged open. Isolde pushed the bench against the wall, stood on top and cranked open the window's casement. She looked out just in time to see Tristin ride through the gates, followed by a dozen of knights on horseback, some wearing partial armor, all carrying lances or other hand weapons. They thundered across the lowered drawbridge.

Over a tunic of deep blue, Tristin wore an armor breastplate that had been polished to brilliance. On his shield was emblazoned the Cornish coat of arms. His stallion was white, draped in a splendid cloth woven with blue and gold thread. Immediately behind him rode three knights each carrying the Cornish flag bearing a bold white cross set against a black background.

Stopping just across the drawbridge, Tristin reigned in his stallion, a spirited horse that pranced in place as if ready to take flight. Tristin held the reigns firm, turned back toward the castle, and looked up at the towers. When he looked directly toward Isolde, her heart beat rapidly. Instinctively she ducked from sight.

Then, summoning her courage, she put her face back to the window. Why shouldn't she look directly at him? After all, if he managed to kill the river creature, he would be escorting her across the sea to Cornwall. They'd see plenty of each other if that happened.

Tristin did not seem to pay any particular attention to her window. Did he see her, she wondered? Did he know she was watching him? He was so handsome she caught her breath. His dark hair hung thickly to his neck, framing his finely chiseled face.

He turned his horse and galloped away with the ease and skill of a natural horseman. What was it about him, she wondered, that filled her with longing and something almost like a sweet sadness? After all she'd seen him only from a distance. When he'd first entered the castle keep two days earlier, she'd watched him from a hiding place on a balcony. When he'd gone out hunting with her father and brothers, she'd watched their riding party gallop away from behind the battlements. What did she know of him, other than that was utterly appealing and the nephew of her future husband?

She pressed her cheek to the cool metal grating and watched until he disappeared from view.

In fact, Tristin *had* seen Isolde in the window, and he guessed immediately who she was from the light golden red of her hair which caught just enough of the hazy sunlight to glow like a halo around her face.

Just a year earlier, Tristin's uncle Mark announced he'd never remarry. He said he was perfectly content to leave his kingdom to his nephew Tristin. He'd put off his noblemen who were anxious about the succession by saying, "I will not remarry unless my bride's eyes are as blue as the summer sky on a perfectly clear morning, and her hair is the color of spun gold tinged with the blush of a rose. And of course she must be every inch a royal princess."

"You jest," said Lord Denoalan, one of his nobles. Finding a royal princess of marriageable age was difficult enough – specifying hair and eye color, particularly such exquisite coloring – was nothing short of unreasonable.

"I do not jest," King Mark had said. "Until such a princess is available to be my bride, I will not remarry."

Soon afterward, Lords Denoalan and Godwin asked permission to leave the court. Mark gave them permission, glad to see them go. They had been making trouble lately, stirring up the old rumor that Tristin was not in fact the legitimate son of Mark's sister, and therefore, not legitimate heir to the Cornish throne.

Four months later, Lords Denoalan and Godwin returned and requested an audience saying they brought a gift which would please the king, a gift which may even alter the course of his life and the destiny of the kingdom.

The kingdom of Cornwall was a wealthy one, with rich deposits of tin and copper. All one had to do was walk along the rocky shores to find tin and copper deposits among the gravel. Fortune seekers came from all over to gather the ore, paying a tax to the Cornish king for any metal they took away with them. As a result, Tintagel's main keep, which also served as a throne room, glittered with opulent luxury. The walls were lined with richly embroidered tapestries of gold, silver, blue and red. The great hall was aisled like a church, with a domed ceiling set with tin panels. On display were full suits of armor of exquisite workmanship. The hall was lit by sunlight coming in through high windows set with glazed glass imported from Rome.

The entire court gathered in the great hall of Tintagel Castle to see the gift Lords Denoalan and Godwin brought. King Mark, sitting on the throne, looked every inch the king, his beard full and dark with a touch of gray at his temples, his hair coarse and thick. He had a battle scar running from his cheek to his forehead. His brows were heavy, threaded with gray. He was lean and muscular, his eyes sharp and intelligent. On his head he wore a crown. Today because the occasion was informal, he wore a small circlet of gold.

Tristin stood in the place of honor nearest the throne, beneath the richly embroidered canopy over the throne proclaiming Mark's royal estate.

The guards at the door announced the arrival of Lords Denoalan and Godwin. The king nodded to the guards, who swung open the doors. Lords Denoalan and Godwin entered and bowed ceremoniously to King Mark. Both men were in their early thirties, both had suspicious natures. Lord Godwin, the taller of the two, turned back and gestured to two pages, who also entered carrying a large canvas wrapped in rose-colored satin.

Lord Godwin unveiled the canvas to reveal a painting of a breathtakingly beautiful girl wearing a gown of pale shimmering green. Her eyes were indeed was the pure luminescent blue of a summer sky on a clear morning. Her hair was like spun gold tinged with a soft blush red. She was slender, with long graceful arms. Her face was all sweetness and sensuous curves – her chin pert and rounded, her nose straight, her lips bow shaped.

King Mark stepped down from his throne and came closer to study the painting. The others – his attendants and knights and lords then in service – also stepped forward for a better view.

"May I present Princess Isolde of Leinster," said Lord Denoalan.

The king was silent for such a long time, his courtiers became restless. All his energy was concentrated on the portrait, his eyes bright, his breathing slow and measured. Others who didn't know or understand the king as well as Tristin probably saw nothing in his carefully impassive face, but Tristin knew that his uncle was powerfully moved.

"I commend the remarkable talent of the painter," the king said at last, "but such a girl can only exist in the imagination of an artist."

"Oh, but she is real," said Lord Godwin softly, "very real. I saw her myself."

"Is the painting a good likeness?" King Mark asked.

"No, my liege," Lord Godwin said. He paused dramatically and said, "It is *not* a good likeness. She is much more beautiful than this."

"How is it that she is not betrothed?" King Mark asked.

"She has only recently reached the age allowing for betrothal."

Mark turned abruptly from the painting and returned to his throne, where he sat very straight. Tristin, seeing his mood, said, "Shall we leave you, my liege?"

"Yes, please," King Mark said.

"What shall I do with the painting?" Lord Godwin asked the king.

"Leave it here."

Tristin didn't have a chance to talk to Mark alone until much later that evening when they sat in the king's private presence chamber playing a game of chess. Like everything else in Tintagel Castle, the chess pieces were of the best quality, cast in bronze and exquisitely sculpted. Mark moved a castle and looked up.

"Will you marry her?" Tristin asked. His tone betrayed nothing except simple curiosity.

"Do you think I should?"

"She is said to be as charming as she is beautiful, so I see no reason why you should not try for her hand. Besides, if you will only have a royal princess with such hair and eyes, you may not have much choice."

"It's your move," said Mark.

Tristin disliked the game of chess, but played it because it was Mark's favorite pastime. The game suited Mark, who was contemplative and inward and thoughtful. Tristin was a man of action who disliked sitting so long. He was often impatient with the game's long silences, and usually lost simply because he lacked the ability to suppress his restlessness long enough to plan as many moves ahead as was necessary to pose even a challenge to so expert a chess player as Mark.

Tristin moved a knight. Instantly Mark took his piece. After a few more moves, when it was clear Tristin had lost the game, Mark said, "There are many who would not understand if you so peacefully accepted my remarriage."

"Why wouldn't I want you to remarry? I'm tired of all the jealousy and back-biting. If you have a son and heir, the succession would be settled as it should be."

"People will still wonder," said Mark.

"Don't forget, if I wanted a dukedom of my own, I could have it. I like it here."

Mark moved his castle and said, "I don't think I should marry her."

"Why not?" asked Tristin, startled.

"She is so young. I don't believe she'd be happy with a man so much older."

"Nonsense. There is nothing old about you. You are the King of Cornwall. Of course she would be happy with you."

"What about you?" Mark asked. "Isn't it time for you to stop fooling around with village girls and find a wife worthy of your station and estate?"

"I have thought about that, too," Tristin said. "One day, perhaps, I shall return to Brittany and find a wife there."

For many days, Tristin and his men hunted along the shores and inland waterways of the River Slanley without catching sight of the creature. They carried longbows, lances, and throwing axes. Swords and regular axes would be useless against so fierce a beast. In each of the villages along the river they asked about the creature. They were regaled by fantastic stories of a beast large enough to destroy a fishing boat, or attack and kill half dozen men at once, but not once did they catch sight of the creature.

Tristin and his men set up camp on a stretch of shore not far from the mouth of the river because they'd been told the creature lived in the ocean but frequently ventured into a small cove near the river's mouth. His men dragged the river bottom with a dragnet and hook, hoping to stir the creature from hiding, and searched along the shores for tracks. By the third day, Tristin began wondering if the creature existed at all.

It was late afternoon and the skies were gray and drizzly. Tristin was on the north shore of the river, not far from the sea, when a boy of about twelve ran toward them.

"There!" cried the boy. "The creature is over there!" He gestured wildly.

The boy wore the ragged undyed woolen garb of a villager belted at the waist, with baggy trousers and with boots laced up to his knees tied in place with metal hooks. He doubled over, out of breath from running, then straightened up and pointed northward toward a finger-shaped pool of water jutting into the rocky shoreline.

Tristin's men, each carrying weapons, some carrying hooks and nets as well, ran where the boy pointed. As they approached the pool, the creature lifted its head from the water. The creature was truly terrifying, with a long but stout neck and a flat head which was mostly jaws, and a long body. Fully extended, the creature was probably twenty feet in length. From its mouth darted a long forked tongue.

With hardly a splash, the creature ducked back into the water. Several of the men cast their net near the opening of the pool to keep the creature from escaping back to the river and out to sea. Two of the men threw their hooks and dragged the hooks along the bottom of the pool to force the creature to rear its head again. The others stood ready on the shore.

When the beast again came partly out of the water, Tristin could see the head was at least two feet long and its forked tongue flickered at least a foot in length. The creature unhinged its jaws and opened its mouth to reveal a row of jagged shark-like teeth.

One of Tristin's men emitted a low, respectful whistle. No wonder the villagers were terrified.

The problem was how to kill it.

The creature was trapped, so there was no time to waste. Tristin gave the command and three of the men let fly their axes, and two shot arrows. Two of the axes missed, but one axe caught the creature in the back. An arrow pierced near a front arm.

With a growl, the animal sprang onto the shore, scuttling on four legs with the quickness and agility of a salamander. The axe in its back and arrow near its arm didn't slow it down at all. The creature was so large the pounding of its feet on the shore sounded like the pounding of drums.

The closest of the men threw spears and lances. With a quick dartlike movement, the creature lunged at the nearest man, who thrust his lance forward and caught the creature near the neck. The lance, like the two axes and arrow, didn't stop the creature, whose jaws unhinged and clamped onto the man's leg.

The other ten sprang forward with their weapons. In closer proximity, more of the weapons and arrows hit their marks. With so many lances and spears piercing the armor-like skin of the reptile, the creature unclasped its jaws and gave a large guttural hiss. But the creature lunged forward as if the spears piercing his back were nothing more than irritating thorns.

The creature turned toward Tristin and lunged – as if it knew that Tristin, with his crested helmet and arms emblazoned in red on his breastplate – was the leader.

Tristin had already thrown his lance. At his belt he had a dagger. He had only a split second to react. His dagger was in his hand so quickly it seemed to have appeared there by magic.

Tristin aimed and hurled the dagger directly toward the creature's face, aiming directly between the eyes.

The dagger hit its mark. The force of the dagger slowed the creature enough so that Tristin could leap out of the way just in time to avoid being swatted by the creature's enormous front paw.

The creature staggered, evidently felled by the dagger. Others threw lances and spears, many of which glanced off his scales which seemed as strong as armor. With the dagger stuck into its forehead, the fearsome head dropped. It refused to give up, though. With another hiss, it made a feeble attempt to leap toward another of the men.

One of Tristin's men still had a dagger. He handed the dagger to Tristin, who aimed again, and once again the dagger entered the beast's forehead. The animal was powerful and fierce enough that it could probably best a full grown bear in hand-to-hand combat, but with the two daggers between its eyes, it rolled over, defeated, onto its back, and lay still.

The village boy, who had been hiding behind a large boulder, crept toward the dead beast. "There's poison in his teeth and claws," said the boy, pale and shaken, "I think it can still kill."

Tristin didn't doubt that. Breathless and dripping with perspiration, he removed his helmet and visor. "Quick," he said, gesturing toward the wounded man, "help him."

Already two of the men were tearing cloth into bandages to stop the injured man's leg from bleeding.

"Quickly," Tristin said to the village boy. "Run to the nearest village and find
someone who knows medicine!"

"Yes, my lord!" the boy cried. He had had been squatting near the injured man. He leaped to his feet, turned and ran, disappearing around the rocky crags.

Already the wounded man was warm with fever. His face was deathly pale, his eyes bloodshot. "My leg is burning," he said. "I felt the heat from the creature's mouth. It does indeed breathe fire."

Those were his last words. He grew paler and weaker by the minute.

It wasn't long before a medicine woman came from the village, followed by other villagers coming behind her, but even Tristin, untrained in medicine, knew there was nothing to be done for the wounded man. His eyes were closed and a putrid smell came from his wound.

The medicine woman knelt beside him, touched his forehead, and examined his wound – which showed the teeth marks and torn flesh – and shook her head sadly. "I've never seen anyone live after being bitten by that monster."

The huge beast lay lifeless on the sand. Taking great care because of the monster's powerful poison, Tristin extracted two of the largest teeth and the longest of the claws to present to the King of Leinster as proof that the creature was dead. The teeth were four inches long, the claws longer than his hand.

Not that proof was needed. The villagers who had followed the medicine woman gathered around to gaze in awe at the monster's body. The boy told them the story of how Tristin had killed the beast by hitting him twice with daggers right between the eyes. Tristin knew it wouldn't be long before the story spread to the far corners of the kingdom.

Isolde and her mother sat in the sun room high in the castle's east tower at work on a piece of beaded embroidery. They worked silently, shoulder to shoulder in straight-backed chairs in front of a large embroidery hoop. On the hoop was mounted a square of finely spun wool nearly covered with exquisite stitches and glass beads. Isolde strung the beads onto a thread while her mother secured them in place with a second needle and thread.

As they worked a village girl sat on a nearby stool, strumming a lute and singing softly. The only other sound was the faint cackling of the fire. The sunlight streamed in through the windows, throwing diamond-patterned shadows from the window grates on the floors and walls.

The late afternoon sun was growing dim when the queen inserted her needle into the fabric and rubbed her hands to soothe them. "Do you know," she said, "that King Mark of Cornwall swore never to marry again."

If this was intended to make Isolde feel better, it didn't. She didn't know King Mark had been married before – although she should have guessed it, given his age.

"Really?" said Isolde politely.

"Indeed," said the queen. "His first queen died after five years of marriage and three stillborn children. One child, a boy, lived for a few months, then died. After that birth, the queen weakened until eventually she, too, died. She was never able to bear a healthy child. Everyone says King Mark loved her deeply and swore never to marry again – until he saw your portrait."

"I'm honored." Isolde gave the dutiful answer, but she didn't feel honored. She felt unlucky. Why couldn't the King of Cornwall be young and dashing, like Tristin?

"We shall all be honored by such a marriage alliance," said the queen.

"But I may not marry King Mark at all," said Isolde, casting about for a graceful way to change the subject. "A difficult and even deadly task was placed before his nephew. Do you really think he will be able to find and kill the river creature?"

"If anyone can do it, his nephew can," said the queen.

Pleased to be talking about Tristin instead of King Mark, Isolde was careful to keep her tone off-hand and casual. "What makes you think that?"

"Tristin has proven himself fierce in battle, many times."

"Please tell me," said Isolde.

"He was a young man in his uncle's court, newly knighted when he returned to his native Brittany to avenge his father's death. His father was duke of Brittany and was murdered by usurpers. King Mark provided the army and weapons, but Tristin led the battle and inspired his men. Within a fortnight he'd killed his father's murderer and reclaimed the duchy."

"Tristin is duke of Brittany?" Isolde asked.

"No, that's one of the strange things about him. He had no desire to remain in Brittany to rule. He conferred the title to the man who raised him until the age of eight, a man who saved his life and hid him from his enemies. He wanted to return to Cornwall to serve his uncle. He is said to be fiercely loyal to his uncle."

"I see," said Isolde. She put a few more careful stitches into the fabric. Surely anyone would see how much more interesting Tristin was than his uncle!

Tristin and his men had been gone now for three days. Each time the drawbridge was raised or lowered – in fact, each time Isolde heard any noise at all – she imagined that he and his men were returning.

Isolde and her mother returned to their embroidery. The light streaming in through the windows was growing weaker so soon they would have to stop.

Then, from the distance came the pounding of horse hooves. Both Isolde and her mother looked at each other. Isolde leapt to her feet and stood up on one of the benches and cranked open the window.

"Isolde," the queen said, "come down! Someone might see you!"

"Oh, but mother—" The troop of knights flying the Cornish flag were galloping toward the castle. Isolde caught her breath. It was just before dusk, the sky luminescent lavender. Already a few stars had come out. In the twilight, the galloping knights looked like beings from another sphere.

"Come *down*, Isolde!"

Isolde stepped from the bench. The queen was standing, too, so they stood facing each other. Isolde was now a few inches taller than her mother, which gave her an unsettling feeling.

"All right," said the queen, "you may as well tell me. What did you see?"

"Tristin and his men are returning."

The queen looked longingly toward the window. Isolde knew she wanted to look outside – but she didn't dare.

"I suppose they've done the deed," the queen said quietly. "They would not be returning this soon otherwise. Unless—"

Unless something bad happened, was what she didn't say.

"They've probably killed it," Isolde said. She felt something like a chill even though the room was warm. This meant she would be sent to Cornwall to marry King Mark. It also meant she would see Tristin again, this time face to face. Her fear was tinged with excitement.

Her mother rang the bell for Brangwain, who, minutes later, hurried in. "Oh, Madam!" she said excitedly. "Tristin and his men are coming! They must have killed the river beast!"

"Please prepare Isolde," said the queen. "I wish for Isolde to enter the throne room with me wearing her gold crown and pink silken gown. You and two of my attendants will follow."

Brangwain bobbed a quick curtsey and said, "Yes, Madam! Of course!"

Tristin and his men stood in the throne room, their helmets tucked under their arms. Isolde and the queen entered walking arm-in-arm, followed by Brangwain and two other attendants. As the queen had commanded, Isolde wore her pink silk gown and small golden crown. The gown shimmered in the bright torchlight. Her hair was brushed loosely around her shoulders, falling down her back in curls.

The crowd of knights parted, creating an aisle so Isolde and the queen could pass. Isolde's father, who had been sitting on his throne, stood up and held out his hand for his wife and daughter to join him on the dais. Also on the dais were Isolde's two older brothers, Daman and Conal.

Isolde walked slowly and gracefully. She was the Princess of Leinster, and she knew how to play the role to perfection. She and the queen reached the dais and climbed the three steps. The king led them to two chairs also beneath the royal canopy – the queen's throne and a chair for Isolde next to her mother. Isolde's chair, like the larger thrones, was intricately carved in wood with a tall back and a cushioned foot rest.

After Isolde was in her chair, she dared looked at Tristin, for the first time seeing him close up. His youthful face had the high color of someone accustomed to vigorous exercise, and the bearing of one eager for adventure. His body was well-proportioned, his torso reminding her of the marble statute her oldest brother had brought back from Rome.

The king handed the queen a silver casket. She opened the casket and drew in her breath sharply. The king said, "Tristin has brought the teeth and claws of the river creature to prove that it has been slain."

"These teeth and claws are truly terrifying," the queen said. To Tristin, she said, "I am grateful to you, and all your men, for ridding our kingdom of this monster."

"I have another casket," said Tristin, "a gift for the princess from King Mark."

He stepped forward and handed the king another casket, this one much smaller, a delicate casket made of highly-polished silver and set with jewels, small enough for a man to enclose entirely in his palm.

The king opened the casket, looked inside, and closed the lid again. "On behalf of my daughter, I accept this gift. You and all your men are welcome to share our evening meal in the great hall. The day after tomorrow, you may escort my daughter and her waiting woman to Tintagel Castle."

Tristin bowed low. "I shall send the good news back to Cornwall at once."

Late that night, after Isolde had gone to bed, the queen called Brangwain into her private chambers and handed her a glass bottle shaped like an onion with a large rounded base and thin neck. "It is a love potion," the queen said.

"A love potion, Madam?"

"I believe it is very strong. It came from the village witch of Rath Luirc."

Brangwain turned the bottle over in her hands, amazed. She pulled out the cork and smelled the liquid, which had the scent of lightly spiced apple wine.

"If it is from the Rath Luirc witch, Madam, I am sure it is very powerful."

"It is powerful, but the effects do not last long."

Brangwain replaced the cork. "What shall I do with it, Madam?"

"You will see that my daughter drinks this the evening of her wedding. I'm very much afraid that she will be unhappy married to a man so much older. But if she drinks this, she will fall madly in love with him, and then she will be happy."

"But you said it doesn't last long!"

"It doesn't need to last long. It needs to last only long enough for her to see and appreciate King Mark's noble qualities."

"Do you think it will work?" Brangwain asked.

"Of course it will work!"

The morning sky was slate gray, the air damp. The entire court gathered to see Princess Isolde and her retinue set off on the short journey from the castle to the ship belonging to the King of Cornwall waiting just off shore.

The retinue and court gathered in the courtyard, just inside the castle's main gates. Isolde and her parents had already said their goodbyes. Now, one last time, Isolde kissed her mother's cheek.

"You will make us proud," her mother whispered.

"I will try," Isolde said.

The king held the bridle of Isolde's horse as she mounted. Her two elder brothers rode on either side of her. Behind came Brangwain. It had been decided that Brangwain would accompany Isolde to Cornwall and stay long enough to help her get settled and accustomed to her new attendants and ladies, then return to Leinster and get married. Behind Brangwain were Tristin's knights. Leading the entire procession was Tristin.

The body of the river creature had been examined closely by dozens of people, including the king of Leinster's own wise men. The creature was conclusively determined to be a reptile. A reptile with fire in its mouth was a dragon. Tristin, therefore, was styled a dragon-slayer and was now a hero throughout Leinster.

A flourish of trumpets sounded and the procession started off across the lowered drawbridge. In the hazy light, the distant hills seemed eerie and somber, glowing purple. The white birches appeared lavender. The road was heavily gutted from the winter rains.

Once they'd ridden most of the way down the hill, Isolde looked back at the castle, at the spires, turrets, and battlements glowing through the mists as if touched by magic. Her parents and the entire court stood watching. She lifted her hand for one last wave. A lump came into her throat, but she held herself proudly, aware she was on display.

She turned forward and watched Tristin at the head of the retinue, mesmerized by how expertly he handled his stallion. The rumbling of so many horse hooves sounded like a rolling of drums or canons. Up ahead, two horsemen carried flags which waved and snapped in the breeze. Her sadness at leaving home and unease with knowing she must marry a stranger fell away, and she felt a sense of excitement and expectation.

To reach the port, they would pass through three villages, the first of which lay at the bottom of the castle hill. The first village consisted of about fifty half-timbered cottages with thatched roofs scattered through the softly rolling hills. The fields, now being plowed for the planting season, spread out beyond the village toward the river.

As the procession passed through the first village, the villagers ran from their fields and homes to wave to Isolde and shout greetings and good wishes. She smiled and waved as they passed. Over the next hill they came to the second village, where she was greeted even more warmly. Here villagers waved the flag of Cornwall and the flag of Leinster. As she passed, they shouted: "Isolde, future queen of Cornwall!"

To Tristin they shouted, "Hail to the dragon-slayer!"

The third village through which they passed was a fishing village. Here the welcome was particularly jubilant because those living along the shore felt the deepest gratitude at being rid of the river creature. The villagers had erected an enormous banner over the road depicting a powerful knight slaying a dragon. The women and children shouted out their thanks to Tristin as he passed.

The procession reached the shore and rode along the firm sand the tide had left smooth in its retreat. Anchored just off shore were was the ship bearing a Cornish flag, waving and snapping in the breeze.

Tristin pulled his horse to a stop and dismounted, as did Isolde's two brothers. All three men came to her horse to help her dismount. Tristin stood back respectfully and allowed her brothers to do the honor. After Isolde dismounted, her brothers ceremoniously walked her to the gangplank.

The oldest of her brothers said to Tristin, "I give my sister, the Princess of Leinster, to your safekeeping."

"I will see that she is safe and well cared for," Tristin said.

Tristin scarcely looked at Isolde. She wondered if he was trying not to look at her, or if he simply had no interest in looking at her.

She turned to hug each of her brothers goodbye. Then she stepped onto the gangplank. The plank rocked, and Isolde felt unsteady on her feet. Stiffly, Tristin offered her his arm. The rocking of the boards and the sharp, salty smell of the sea made her feel light-headed. Carefully she walked along the boards to the ship.

Once the entire retinue was on board, two men cranked up the anchor, and two others pulled the gangplank onto the ship. Isolde's brothers and their grooms stood on the shore, waving. Also on the shore were dozens of villagers and fisher families who followed the procession to watch the royal retinue.

The ship set sail and Isolde stood at the railing watching as the shoreline grew smaller and at last faded from view. Brangwain stood beside her.

"Princess Isolde," came a man's voice from behind her. She knew without turning that the speaker was Tristin. She'd heard his voice only once before, but who could forget the richness of it?

She turned and there he was, standing a respectful distance.

"Perhaps," he said, "you and your maid would like to see your cabins."

"I would, thank you," said Isolde. "But perhaps Brangwain prefers to remain on deck a while longer."

If Brangwain understood the hint, she ignored it. "I would like to see our cabins as well," she said.

"This way," Tristin said. He led them to a ladder. When he gripped Isolde's elbow to help her down the short narrow ladder, she felt another rush of warmth. Her arm brushed against his chest.

At the bottom of the ladder was a narrow corridor. To the left, the corridor was shorter. At the end were two doors opposite each other.

He led them to the doors and said, "These cabins are for you. These are the only cabins with portholes, the best cabins on the ship. The larger one, of course, is for the princess."

He opened one of the doors and allowed Isolde and Brangwain to look inside. The cabin was just large enough for a bed which was no wider than a few planks. The cabin was scarcely big enough for two people to stand inside. Isolde had expected to share a bed with Brangwain but these planks which passed for a bed could scarcely hold one person.

The other was even smaller. The beds in both cabins were equipped with a leather strap with a metal buckle.

"What is that strap for?" Brangwain asked.

"To keep you from being tossed off the bunk during the night," Tristin said. To Princess Isolde, he said, "You may wish to lie down for awhile. The motion of the ship is easier to take that way. When you become accustomed to the motion of the ship, you can move about freely."

Isolde wanted to look directly into his face, but she was afraid to with Brangwain standing nearby and watching her so closely.

"I think I *will* rest in here for a few minutes," Isolde said. "Thank you."

"I will have your things brought down to you," said Tristin.

Isolde closed the door to her cabin. The room smelled of salty air and something fresh and with the tang of citrus. The porthole was set with heavily leaded glass, so the slight streaming in was gray and weak. The walls were unpolished golden-colored wood.

First she sat on the bunk, but the swaying of the ship made her queasy, so she laid down and closed her eyes.

A few minutes later, a knock came at the door. Isolde sat up and said, "Enter."

The door opened and Tristin stood on the threshold, carrying three of her trunks and Brangwain's smaller leather bags. He'd said he would send someone to bring her things, but here he was, bringing them himself.

He put the trunks and Brangwain's bags on her floor. She was startled by a clunking sound as he put the smaller of Brangwain's bags on the floor. She watched as Tristin secured the trunks with leather straps mounted to the floor boards.

He picked up Brangwain's bag. She said, "Please leave it here."

"Certainly," he said, and put the bag down again. There was that clunk again.

She looked back at him. His eyes were deep blue, bristled with black lashes, his face finely chiseled. Both held perfectly still, watching each other. Isolde's heart beat so furiously she felt faint.

She felt a sudden terror that he would turn and leave and she'd never again be able to talk to him entirely alone. She searched quickly for something to say. "The fogs are heavy," she said, "but the moon tonight will be almost full."

"Indeed, Princess," he said. "The moon may be bright enough that your cabin may never be in complete darkness."

"I've never seen a full moon from the deck of a ship. Perhaps I will venture onto the deck tonight."

He looked at her, startled. "Tonight—? But, I really don't think—"

She looked directly into his eyes and smiled. Her smile had the effect she intended. He entirely froze, as if forgetting what he planned to say next. This man who was so steady in battle that he could throw a lance and hit a dragon right between the eyes was now flustered with a bright pink color in his cheeks.

"You must stay here where you will be safe," he said.

"I shall not be safe on the deck? What if you are there?"

He started to speak, but stopped. Indeed, he *was* flustered.

"I shall walk on deck," she said, "when the moon rises."

He looked at her, alarmed. "But, Princess—"

Just then came the sound of footsteps on the ladder. It was one of Tristin's men who said, "We need on you deck, Tristin."

To Isolde, he said, "I will send your supper down to you later."

She tried to read his expression, but could not. He seemed bewildered or even distressed. His expression, so different from what she hoped to see in his face, caused her eyes to sting with tears of disappointment.

Seeing her tears, he said, "Princess?"

She turned away, too proud to let him see her tears. He touched her shoulder gently. She turned back to him and found herself again looking directly into his eyes.

He whispered, "You are so lovely."

Then he rose, bowed low, and stepped from her cabin, closing the door behind him.

The moment he was gone, she unstrapped Brangwain's bag and looked inside. At the bottom of the bag, she found the onion-shaped bottle of what she assumed was wine, and a sealed letter addressed in her mother's handwriting to King Mark. Curious, Isolde broke the seal and read the letter:

"To his majesty, Mark of Cornwall: This jug contains a magical love potion. Whoever drinks this potion will fall madly in love. The potion lasts only a short time, which will be long enough for my daughter to overcome her maiden shyness and warm to a husband who treats her gently. This potion is my gift for your wedding night. Please keep the secret from my daughter; she does not always approve of magical potions."

Isolde quickly felt in her waistband for the key to her trunks, and opened the larger trunk. Her clothes were neatly folded, smelling of the sweet herb pouches a servant had tucked inside. The bottle was small enough to fit into the trunk's inner compartment. She put the bottle inside, then locked her trunk and refastened the strap.

She had barely gotten back to her bunk when another knock came at the door and Brangwain said, "Isolde? May I come in?"

"Yes, of course," Isolde said.

Brangwain came in and closed the door. "Are you all right? You look sick!"

"I feel sick!" Isolde lied.

"Shall I loosen your waistband so you can rest more comfortably?"

"Yes," Isolde said. "Thank you."

She stood up while Brangwain loosened the ties.

"Tristin was right," Brangwain said. "The rocking motion will be easier to take if we are lying down." She guided Isolde to the bed and pulled a light sheet up to her shoulders.

"I think I'd like to be alone for a while," Isolde said.

Brangwain picked up her bags from the floor and went into her own cabin. Isolde closed her eyes, trying to accustom herself to the rocking motion. She was uneasy, her stomach rolling like the ship. Soon she drifted into a light sleep which was mostly dreamless except for fleeing images of the Tristin's blue eyes, and an onion-shaped bottle filled with a love potion.

Some time later she heard a knock. She sat up and blinked the sleep from her eyes. She was about to ask who it was, then realized the knock was at Brangwain's door and not hers.

Brangwain must have asked who was there because someone in the corridor said, "I am bringing supper for you and the Princess."

"Enter," Brangwain called.

Isolde waited. A few moments later, Brangwain knocked on Isolde's door. "I have our meal." Isolde sat up as Brangwain came in. Isolde could see from her rumpled hair and her loosened gown that she, too, had been resting. Brangwain sat near Isolde on the bunk and put the tray between them. The tray contained spiced meat, a loaf of herb bread with a thick crust, and a bottle of fresh water.

"Did you sleep?" Isolde asked.

"No. I tried, but my stomach was too uneasy." Brangwain looked at the food and said, "I may manage a few bites of the plain bread, but that will be all."

Isolde's head now felt remarkably clear. She realized she felt no sea-sickness at all. She found, though, that she wasn't hungry. She picked at the bread and ate a few bites.

"How are you feeling?" Brangwain asked.

"Not well," Isolde lied. "I may not want to move at all for the next three days."

"Laying flat is best for motion sickness. So just stay on your bunk."

"I will," Isolde lied again.

When they finished their supper, Brangwain put the tray into a bin in the corridor and returned to her own cabin. Left alone again, Isolde lay still, looking at the rapidly darkening porthole. The moon, she knew, would not rise until after midnight.

She wondered whether she dared go on the deck in the middle of the night. Soon she would be married to a man she already thought of as old and dreary. If she didn't have an adventure now, when would she ever possibly have one?

Tristin slept for a few hours after supper, and was now wide awake, wondering if Isolde might be on the deck of the ship in the dead of night. Earlier he had thought she must have been toying with him and had no such intentions. In fact, he'd been startled out of his senses when she looked directly into his eyes and said she intended to walk on deck after moonrise.

There was no porthole in his cabin so he wasn't sure the hour. Suppose, just suppose, the princess was up on deck, by herself. The idea that harm could come to her while she was entrusted to his care filled him with such fear that he rose to his feet, pulled on his boots and a cape for warmth, and crept from his cabin to the corridor.

As stealthily as a cat, he climbed the ladder to the deck. The deck was sixty paces from bow to stern. Up front was a square platform surrounded by battlements extending out over the stern, where three sailors remained on duty at all times, keeping the masts and sails in proper position. In the stern was another elevated deck, also surrounded by battlements. The moon had just recently risen, so if she'd come on deck even a quarter of an hour earlier, the deck would have been entirely in shadows.

The deck seemed deserted. To make sure, he walked the perimeter.

"Tristin?"

He looked around.

"I'm here."

Isolde was on one of the three smaller raised platforms, a platform fenced with a battlement-topped wall about five feet high. She was nestled in a corner, wrapped in a fur cloak for warmth with a piece of canvas, which looked like part of a sail, pulled over her legs for added warmth.

"What on earth — ?"

"The moon is lovely from here."

"You should be in your cabin!"

She didn't answer. The only sound was the snapping of the sails overhead and the sound of the sea. Then, with something like laughter in her voice, she said, "You should be in your cabin, too!"

He climbed the small ladder to the platform. "Princess Isolde," was all he could manage to say.

Her face, in the moonlight, framed by her golden hair, was a dizzying sight. Her eyes were large and round. She was watching him closely. What he saw in her eyes startled him as much as her invitation. There was a pleading in her eyes, something like a deep need, as if there was something she wanted from him. Instinctively he moved toward her.

He sat beside her, leaning back against the platform wall, which was high enough to hide them from anyone walking by the deck. He sat a few feet away from her, afraid if he sat any closer, he would entirely forget himself.

"We've never really talked, you know," she said.

"We haven't," he agreed. His throat felt suddenly tight, his entire body warm.

"I brought something," she said, patting a velvet purse tied to her waistband with a golden rope. From the purse she pulled out a bottle of what he assumed was wine.

"Please drink some of this with me," she said and pulled out the cork. He could smell the wine, a mixture of honey and apples and spices. She took a sip and handed him the bottle.

He drank deeply from the bottle. The wine stirred him, and he was already off balance. "This is unusual wine," he said.

"Yes," she said. "Very."

He felt entirely captivated. All he could do was stare at her. There were but a few feet between them. If she were anyone other than Princess Isolde of

Leinster, he would reach for her and pull her against him. The very thought of doing so made him feel weak and giddy. He drank more of the wine, which made him even more lightheaded.

He set the bottle down. She was not a village girl to be trifled with. She was a royal princess whose safety and care had been entrusted to him. He knew they should both return to their cabins immediately, but he sat without moving. The moon was high enough now large and luminous and white to bathe her face in silvery glow.

"Do you feel anything different?" she asked.

"Different? The wine is certainly unusual tasting. What do you mean by different?"

She licked her lips as if to remove any vestiges of wine. The sight of her darting tongue caused a wave of heat to pour through him.

"Do you feel love?" she asked again.

Love?

His heart was pounding. Summoning all his self control, he spoke from duty, "I feel the love a loyal knight should feel for his future queen, and the lady soon to become his aunt by marriage."

To his own ears, his voice sounded uncertain and weak.

"That is not what you are supposed to feel. You are supposed to feel love."

"I did not need the wine for that," he said. "Who could not feel love, Isolde, sitting here so close to you? But tell me, why is drinking this wine supposed to make me feel love?"

She looked into the jug to see how much remained, then said, "I will tell you after you drink some more."

He reached for the bottle and took a long drink. "All right. Tell me. Where did you get the wine?"

"It isn't wine."

He felt an actual rush of fear. His heart pounded so violently he felt a rush like waves hitting the shore. "What is it, Princess?"

"It is a love potion. Anyone who drinks it will fall madly in love."

He looked into her face, deeply confused by her large and glowingly beautiful blue eyes and the soft appealing curves of her face. She leaned toward him and he smelled something light and powdery.

"You want me to fall in love with you?" His words came out as a hoarse whisper.

She watched him closely, but didn't answer. Whether it was the wine, or her nearness, or need in her eyes, he didn't know. His resistance fell away completely and he reached for her. She leaned toward him and their lips met. On her lips he tasted the spices of the wine. He gripped her more tightly, and she tipped her head back.

Summoning every ounce of his self-control, he pulled away and said, "We cannot do this."

"Do what?" she asked. Then she smiled. "What shall we do?" A teasing note crept into her voice. "Or what shall we not do?"

The moon was so bright he could see her face as clearly as if she they were in a candlelit room, which, combined with the radiance of her hair, gave her an unearthly look, as if she were a heavenly being. The wine and the moonlight and the intoxicating closeness of this glowingly beautiful girl so befuddled him that he literally forgot who she was, and who he was. He was aware of nothing except her nearness, the softness of her skin, and the heat pouring into his pulsating loins.

He kissed her again, more deeply this time. Through his light-headed and dazed confusion, he thought she had cast a spell on him. The magic in that wine was too powerful for him to fight. He knew from her responses, shocked at first, then tentative, that she'd never been kissed this way before. He gripped her tighter and forced her mouth to open. She melted into him.

Isolde realized with amazement that she felt no fear. She hadn't really believed the potion was a love potion. She knew the witch of Rath Luirc and she hadn't really believed the potion would work. But now, as his arms tightened around her and she felt crushed against him, she looked up at his face and she knew from the intensity in his expression, face almost as if he were in physical pain, that the potion *had* worked. She was so relieved to see that he desired her, and that his love rendered him helpless, that she realized with a start that this was as far as she had planned. All she had wanted was for this magnificent man to drink the potion and fall in love with her.

Now what?

Here she was, alone with him in the dark in a hidden corner of the ship. His hands were in her hair, stroking her neck and back. Overhead, a gust of wind rattled the sails, causing them to snap and blow. He tipped her face back, kissing her again. Then he bent lower and kissed her neck. She squirmed. His kisses became more insistent, more dizzying. He pulled her so close that she felt the powerful muscles of his arms, torso, and legs. She felt helpless and warm and excited all at the same time. Next his hands were on her legs, groping until he pushed aside her skirts and found her bare legs.

With his hands sliding up her thighs, she felt her first moment of fear. But she was too overwhelmed by the shocking sensations all through her body to think clearly about what they were doing – or to care.

She was still with him, cradled in his arms, when the first light of dawn showed in the east. She felt drowsy and languid and deliriously happy. She was therefore startled when he looked toward the east, and drew himself up with a start, and said, "You must get back to your cabin!"

She was not at all sure she must get back to her cabin, but after the hours they had just spent together, she felt powerless to doubt or question him. He pulled his clothing back into place, evidently expecting her to do the same. He handed her the onion-shaped bottle.

"We must hurry," he said. "It is likely that some members of my crew know we are here. They will perhaps remain silent from loyalty to me."

The ship was still enveloped in darkness when they crept across the deck back to the hatch leading below. He swiftly opened the hatch and helped her down. When they stepped down from the latter, he whispered "That love potion must have been very strong to make us so forget ourselves!"

She felt a hurt as intense as if her heart had been physically squeezed. "You don't love me anymore?" she asked. She felt tears coming to her eyes.

Instantly he melted. "Of course I do. But what can change? Nothing can change. You are the Princess of Leinster. You are betrothed to my uncle!"

He took her elbow and led her back to her cabin. When they reached her cabin, he opened the door for her. She stepped inside, holding the bottle. Before he could close the door, she whispered fiercely, "I will be back on the deck tonight, when the moon is high. You will come back, I know you will!"

Then she flung herself onto her bed and buried her face under her arms.

He closed the door quietly and walked away so stealthily she heard no footsteps at all. Soon dawn lit the window and filled her cabin with a hazy light. She looked around and thought how different everything seemed. Well, why wouldn't everything look different? She herself felt entirely changed. Never had she imagined that love was so exquisite, so intense, an unexpected force coupled with surprising tenderness.

She drifted to sleep, utterly content, and sure that if Tristin didn't already love her as much as she loved him, he soon would. Her confidence did not come from the fact that he drank the potion. Her confidence came from the sheer strength of her wish and desire. How could he not respond in kind?

She awoke to a light knocking at her door. "Who is there?" she asked.

"It's me, Brangwain. I have breakfast for you."

Brangwain! Isolde turned toward the wall and closed her eyes, fearing that Brangwain would know the truth the moment she looked at her. How could she not? Isolde felt so utterly transformed by her experiences in Tristin's arms, how would Brangwain, who had known her so many years, not see it instantly?

Isolde hid the onion-shaped bottle under her blankets. "Come in," she said.

Brangwain opened the door and entered. The cabin was so small Isolde could feel the brush of Brangwain's clothing against her. She kept her face to the wall.

"Are you all right?" Brangwain asked.

"I am not well," said Isolde, afraid to show her face.

Brangwain held perfectly still. There was no movement at all. Isolde hardly breathed.

"You smell like perspiration and –"

Isolde waited in fear. Did love have a *smell*? Could Brangwain smell what she and Tristin had done just a few short hours before?

"Maybe if I sleep some more I will feel better," said Isolde.

"You don't want breakfast?"

"Not now," Isolde said, although in fact she felt hungry. "Please leave some food and let me rest."

Brangwain leaned over and touched Isolde's forehead. "You don't feel feverish. You probably have a touch of seasickness."

Isolde listened as Brangwain put something down on the floor. "I will be back in a little while, to see if you are better," Brangwain said.

Isolde did not respond. Brangwain left, closing the door behind her.

Tristin was too restless to remain in his cabin. As a rule, he hated being confined to a ship. Ordinarily, in such a mood, he'd go hunting. Vigorous exercise always calmed him and focused his thinking. As it was, he was tormented, simply tormented, by memories of how Isolde had moved in his arms, how she had looked up at him with those magnificent eyes, how she had nestled her cheek against him, how had clung to him, yielding to his caresses. The memories filled him with a desire more urgent then he'd ever felt before in his life.

It was that potion, he thought. It had to be. Her beauty was great, no doubt, but only a magical potion could have so bewitched him that even now he felt overcome by a desire to hurry back to her cabin and take her into his arms again forgetting everything, including his honor and duty to his uncle.

Needing to do something, he went to join his men on the deck. With the sea captain he checked the position of the sea.

"At this speed," the captain said, "we should reach Cornwall day after tomorrow."

"That is good," Tristin said mechanically. He looked in the direction of Cornwall, but found himself thinking about the softness of Isolde's touch, the smell of her hair, the luxuriousness of her body, the way she had moved under him. He shook his head. Remember was maddening.

Mark had said it was time to stop fooling around with village girls and find a wife suitable to his rank and station. Indeed, how could he ever again settle for less than a girl of such beauty, her skin so soft and cared for, her hair luxurious, her breath sweet? The difference between a princess and a village girl was indeed the difference between wine and water.

Twice during the day he napped, otherwise, he kept himself busy – helping his crew, steering the ship, seeing that all was in order – but it did not help. The deck was too small. He was constantly aware that at any moment Isolde might appear, and then what would he do? How could he see her without wanting to sweep her into his arms? How could he see her without both of them giving everything away in the way they looked at each other?

After supper with his crew on deck, he returned to his cabin and, soon after the sun set, he fell asleep. With a jolt, he awoke a few hours later. He pulled on his boots and cloak and went onto the deck. The moon had not yet risen so the deck was dark. He felt his way around the perimeter of the deck.

He reached the enclosed raised platform where he'd found her the night before and whispered, "Isolde?"

"I am here."

The air rushed from his lungs in a deep sigh. His body already burned with desire. He felt his way along the platform until he reached her. Instantly, she put her arms around his neck and pressed against him.

In the thin moonlight he could see the tinge of apricot on her cheek, and the bristling of her black lashes touching her cheek. There was such sweetness in her face, and such plaintive love that he tipped back her head and kissed her.

Immediately he sensed a change in her. Last night she'd been tentative, meekly following his lead, moving gently underneath. Now she responded with an urgency and passion matching his own, clinging tightly to him and moaning softly. Now she followed his lead with the grace and assurance of a dancer.

Much later, he cradled her head in the crook of his elbow. Softly, he said, "Late tomorrow, we will arrive at Tintagel Castle."

"And I will have to marry King Mark."

She buried her face against his shoulder, and put her hands around his neck to pull him closer. Just when he thought nothing else she might say or do would shock him, she said, "But you do not want to run away with me?"

Astonished, he pulled back and looked at her. "Run away with you?"

"Do you not love me?"

"Of course I love you! How could I not? But run away, Isolde? Where would we go? How would we live? Your father is a king with a mighty army. He will believe I have abducted you. My uncle is a king with an even mightier army."

"But if I say I went with you of my own free will—" She broke off and looked at him.

He closed his eyes and imagined having her with him forever. What more would he ever want? Surely they could find a place to live. Perhaps he could bring her to Brittany.

He sighed. "Who will believe I did not seduce you? Nobody will believe it. To seduce and abduct a virgin of your rank and station is punishable by death. There is nobody who would have mercy. No knight would align himself with me, should I run away with the princess betrothed to the King of Cornwall. I would not be able to raise an army to defend myself."

She buried her face against his neck. The scent of her and touch of her satiny skin stirred him again. He whispered, "What we have done is dangerous."

"I know," she whispered back. "But we are here now. We have time left tonight. You can still love me more."

Yes. He could do that. And he did.

"What have you done, Isolde?" Brangwain demanded.

Isolde found it difficult to wake up. The moment she'd returned to her cabin just before dawn, she'd fallen into a deep, languid, contended sleep, her body still aglow from lovemaking. She found it difficult to shake off her deep sleepiness even with Brangwain shaking her gently.

"Isolde, please wake up."

Isolde did not want to wake up, particularly to Brangwain's insistent tone. She squinted her eyes open. Brangwain was standing beside her bunk, holding the love potion jug. "Someone drank almost all of this!" Brangwain said.

Isolde sat up, hugging her blankets around her. Brangwain said down next to her.

"Did you drink it?" Brangwain was genuinely alarmed.

Isolde looked directly at Brangwain, "Yes. I did."

"Did you drink it alone?"

Isolde closed her eyes. Unable to help herself, a memory, both delightful and intense, came back to her and she remembered how she had felt, writhing in Tristin's arms. Something like a smile came to her.

"I knew it!" said Brangwain. "I thought there was something strange about the way both you and Tristin were behaving yesterday. You were with him, weren't you! Tell me the truth, please!"

"Yes," said Isolde. She was now fully awake. "I was. We drank the wine together."

"It wasn't wine. It was a love potion."

"Oh, well then," Isolde said with a mischievous smile. "That explains everything that happened afterward."

"Oh, Isolde! This is terrible. What are you going to do when King Mark discovers you're not a virgin?"

The question brought Isolde up sharp. She was so ignorant of these matters. "How will he know?"

"He will know, Isolde. Of course he will know."

Just before dusk, a cry came from the lookout perch high on the main mast. "Land, ho!"

At the cry of land, Isolde squinted, looking as hard as she could. She saw nothing except the sea. There was sudden a flurry of activity as the crew worked the sails. One of the sailors said, "With enough wind we can reach the cove before nightfall."

Soon Isolde saw the distant outline of the shore. As they drew nearer, dusk was falling, but she could see the steep rocky crags and cliffs of the coastline. By the time the crew lowered the anchor, night had almost descended. On the shore, a full retinue was waiting, troops of liveried horsemen wearing brightly colored tunics and crested helmets, their flags waving and snapping in the breeze.

Two men set off from the shore in a rowboat and rowed toward their ship. When the rowboat reached the ship, Tristin came up behind Isolde and said, "Princess Isolde, may I escort you to the king's officers?"

She turned and looked into his face and understood that the formality of his voice was nothing more than a cover. In his eyes was the passion she'd seen the night before. She took his arm and said, "Of course."

He led her to a rope ladder that had been dropped into the rowboat. She climbed down the ladder, followed by Brangwain. The men in the rowboat guided her into the small boat, which rocked perilously on the waves.

"Welcome to Cornwall, Princess Isolde," said one of the officers wearing heavy gold chain with a medallion which Isolde assume designated an official position. At his waist was strapped a long cup-hilted rapier.

She and Brangwain sat close together for warmth as the men rowed them toward the shore. Once on the shore, three men dismounted and bowed to her and also welcomed her to Cornwall.

There were enough horses for Isolde, Brangwain, Tristin and all his men. It took some time, though, for Isolde to feel steady enough on her feet to mount a horse. By the time she mounted, other rowboats reached the shore bearing Tristin's other knights.

They set off northward toward the castle, along the shoreline. To her right were magnificent cliffs. To her left, the ocean beat against the rocky shore. In the twilight, the cliffs appeared purple. Even in twilight, the ocean was a luminescent turquoise green color. The rocky cliffs were also overgrown with a soft carpeting of moss which appeared springy to the touch. The sharp and pungent smell of the ocean brought her a wave of homesickness.

Tristin rode in the lead. Isolde rode not far behind, surrounded on all sides by a royal liveried guard. She knew from the straight line of Tristin's back and the proud tilt of his head that he was deliberately not turning back.

Before long, the steep cliffs came right up to the ocean, making riding along the shore impossible. The retinue turned inland and took a trail through a windswept heath. They rode for some distance before the castle appeared on a distant hilltop, square and imposing and regal, outlined in silhouette against the darkening sky. The trail wound up the castle hill, the steady hoof beats of the horses as constant and lulling as the pitching of a ship.

As they approached she could see that castle was topped with battlements, with squat towers in each corner. In the deepening darkness, the candlelight from within the castle glowed yellow, lighting the arched windows.

A flourish of trumpets sounded, followed by a roll of drums. The castles gates swung open. Just inside was a courtyard, brightly lit by torches in metal holders, hung with banners and flags. Mounted just over the doorway to the main keep was an emblem bearing royal Leinster coat of arms entwined with the royal Cornish coat of arms.

Liveried servants came forward to take their horses. Tristin swung down from his horse and helped Isolde dismount. No sooner had the riders dismounted when there came another flourish of trumpets and the large double arched doors to the castle opened and a man stroke into the courtyard, followed by dozens of courtiers, the women wearing brightly colored silks, some with cone-shaped hats, others with their hair loose in curls, the men smartly dressed with ceremonial cup-hilted rapiers by their sides.

Isolde knew instantly that the man in the lead was King Mark. He wore a small ceremonial gold crown, his beard was closely trimmed, his brows dark and heavy. It was his manner and bearing, even more so than his crown, which gave him away as the king. He strode purposefully into the courtyard like a man born to rule.

Seeing her, he smiled. Not waiting for formal introductions, he walked toward her and reached for her hands. The riders standing nearby stepped back to give them privacy.

His face was exactly what she expected –slightly worn, the face of a man who had known suffering, but the face of a quiet, firm, and gentle man.

"Princess Isolde," he said, his voice was surprisingly rich and melodious. "You are every bit as lovely as your portrait. Welcome. My kingdom is yours."

"Thank you, my lord."

"Come. The ceremony will be brief and we will have a light super. If you feel well enough we can dine with the inner court, otherwise, we can dine in private."

Isolde knew exactly how to conduct herself. After all, had she not been trained for this from birth? In a soft, melodious voice, she said, "We shall do whatever you wish."

He offered her his arm. She took his arm and walked with him across the courtyard, through the arched gates. There, outside the church door, was a crowd so large she thought there were hundreds of people, each of them holding a lit candle. The crowd parted as the king and Isolde walked to the chapel door.

A priest came, wearing flowing robes of finely spun cotton dyed a shimmering black. The priest chanted Latin for so long Isolde began to feel dizzy. Then she and Mark exchanged vows. Quietly he said, "I receive you as mine, so that you become my wife, and I your husband."

It was her turn now. "I receive you as mine," she said, surprised by the sound of her own voice, which was soft and clear, "so that you become my husband, and I your wife." The wedding band the king slipped on her finger was exquisitely worked golden braids set with emeralds and rubies.

The ceremony was over. He took her arm and led her back through the courtyard, through another arched doorway which led into the castle's main keep. "I will show you your new home," he said quietly.

They entered the main keep. She was awed by the grandeur of the room. Hundreds of wax candles were set in glass chandeliers, the flickering flames reflected in tall mirrors mounted through the hall. At the head of the room was a raised dais.

Isolde should have expected such a fabulous display of wealth. She knew, of course, that Cornwall was much larger and wealthier than Leinster, but it wasn't until this moment, standing in this splendid room with so many lit candles that she was struck by the prestige and importance of her new title.

In the next instant, a memory came back of what she and Tristin had done hidden on the ship's platform. Without realizing what she was doing, she turned and looked around.

"Are you looking for your maid?" Mark asked.

"Yes, my lord." How easily she lied!

"She has gone to the set of rooms that will be yours with a full staff of waiting women and servants with instructions to make the rooms comfortable for you. Those were my instructions. Because she knows your tastes and needs, I felt she would be able to direct the servants."

She looked at him, astonished by such kindness. "Thank you, my lord."

"I am sure you must be very tired," he said, "so I will keep our tour brief, but I would like to show you around the castle so that you might feel comfortable here right away. Naturally, anything you wish is a command to be obeyed instantly."

Again, she said, "Thank you, my lord."

"This way," he said "is the state dining room." He led her into a room paneled with darkly polished wood. The room smelled of lemon and wax candles. The floor rushes here, as in the main corridor, were strewn with flower petals and herbs. Three trestle tables each large enough to sit at least fifty people were placed in a U shape. The center table was raised on a dais. Over the two largest chairs was mounted a golden cloth bearing the Cornish coat of arms.

"I have a smaller dining room as well," he said, "upstairs near my private chambers. You also have your own dining room large enough to seat ten. Given how long your journey was and how tired you must be, I shall order a light supper served in my smaller dining room with a just a few of my closest companions. Now I will show you your private apartments."

He led her to a circular stair tower much like the stair towers at Leinster Castle, but these had real glass in the window so the tower wasn't much colder than the main rooms. Up two flights of steps was a landing with two doors in the shape of pointed arches.

"This door is to my chambers," he said. "Our rooms are also joined by a back passageway."

She was startled, although of course she shouldn't have been. At the idea of her sleeping chambers being connected with his, she flushed deeply.

Mark noticed her blushes and wondered about them. He was a close observer by nature, and a shrewd judge of character, often catching small clues that others missed. For example, something in the furtive way she avoided looking at him told him these were not maidenly blushes borne of bashfulness, but instead something else. Dislike of him, perhaps? When he mentioned the back passageway joining their chambers, she gave a start that made him think of guilt.

"Your chambers are in here," he said, opening the door to the right of the landing. He watched her face as he opened the door to her antechamber, and he saw that she was awed and impressed, as she had been with the castle thus far. He'd ordered her chambers furnished and decorated lavishly but tastefully, with both splendor and elegance. The large presence chamber was perfect for evening games with her ladies. One table with a polished marble top was laid with a fine chess board. Two comfortable chairs upholstered with damask and silk cushions stood near enough the large hooded fireplace to offer warmth and comfort. A cluster of other chairs were gathered around a low wooden table for conversation. The walls were paneled with wainscoting and hung with tapestries. The room itself, strewn with fresh rushes, smelled faintly of citrus and flowers.

"It's lovely," she said.

Yes, something was amiss. He could sense it in her bearing. She was impressed with the castle, and pleased with the preparations made for her, but she had trouble looking him in the eye and he didn't understand why.

He opened the door leading to her bedchamber. Again he watched her face and he saw that, as before, she was pleased and impressed. The bed was large and curtained, hung with the finest brocades. The sheets and pillows were made of silk and finely woven cotton. There was a dressing table with two stools, a large imported mirror with a gilded frame.

"Through here," he said, "is a small room where your personal maid can sleep. And over here is your wardrobe room." Even before he opened the door, they could hear the sound of ladies talking softly and laughing. He opened to door and inside was a closet lined with hooks and cupboards. Brangwain was inside, along with a number of others.

Brangwain, seeing Isolde, smiled broadly. "Is this castle not wonderful!"

"Indeed it is," Isolde said.

Just then there came a knock at the main entrance to Isolde's chambers. Mark thought it was a good chance to leave Isolde with her maid and ladies for a few moments, hoping perhaps she would grow more comfortable.

At the door was Geoff, his head steward and one of his most trusted servants. "I came for your next orders, sire," Geoff said.

"I will have supper served in the smaller dining hall. Invite only the members of the inner court."

"Yes, sire."

Mark returned to his own private rooms and closed the door so he could be alone. He sat in his favorite chair positioned near enough to the window to look out, and near enough to the fireplace for warmth. He leaned back, formed his fingers into something like a steeple, bowed his head, and closed his eyes. Giving his eyes a rest was always a relief.

"Is he not handsome?" Brangwain whispered excitedly to Isolde. Their first chance to be alone came when Isolde asked for Brangwain to help her dress for supper, and excused her other attendants.

Isolde sighed deeply but didn't answer.

"You are very lucky." Brangwain took care to whisper softly so that no eavesdroppers could hear. "Next to King Mark, Tristin is a nothing, mere boy, a child."

"How can you say that? He fought a dragon and killed it! That wasn't even his greatest victory in battle! Mere boys don't accomplish such feats."

"Isolde, listen to me. I saw how King Mark looked at you. You have his love, but you can easily lose it, and think what a misery your life will be! You must move forward now and not look back. You must think of what happened on the ship as a mistake. You must forget about it!"

Isolde sank into a chair and buried her face in her hands. Tears came to her, slowly at first. She tried to stifle her sobs but couldn't. How on earth would she get through this? How could she give her body to one man while she was in love with another?

A soft knock came at the door. One of Isolde's attendants called through the door, "Your majesty? Supper will soon be served."

Your *majesty*? Isolde gave a start. Then she remembered. She was now a queen.

Brangwain whispered. "You must dry your eyes and put on a smile. Here, wash your face in this basin."

When Isolde and Brangwain entered the dining room, the room was already filled with people. The moment Isolde entered everyone – including King Mark – stood up. The knights removed their hats. The ladies curtseyed.

Mark sat at the center table beneath a cloth of state. The chair for her, as intricately carved as

Mark's own, was placed to Mark's right. Tristin sat to his left. Tristin had changed from traveling cloak and boots into court attire. At his waist was a ceremonial rapier, his shirt was white and made of finely spun cotton, his trousers black velvet. For just a moment their eyes met and instantly she felt the familiar, intense yearning. She looked away when she felt the color come into her face, terrified that anyone looking at her would understand how she was feeling.

Oh, but Brangwain was wrong! Tristin was magnificent.

Isolde lifted her chin and instinctively stepped into her expected role, smiling and inclining her head graciously. Everyone remained standing as she walked to the center table and stepped upon the dais. Mark came to her with his hand outstretched, and guided to her chair.

Once she sat, everyone else sat as well. The side doors opened and servants entered carrying trays. To her surprise, she was served first, and Mark second. Seeing her startled expression, Mark smiled warmly and touched her hand. She gave a start at his touch. Once everyone had been served, she realized they were waiting for her to eat first. She looked questioningly at Mark. He broke a piece of his own bread, and gave her half.

She took a bite, then the others ate as well. She sipped from her goblet and found to her delight it was pear cider, her favorite. As they ate, hounds sniffed under the tables, pawing through the rushes for scraps or crumbs. Isolde was painfully aware of Tristin seated on the king's other side but she didn't dare look at him again.

A lute player entered. The king gave the command and the lute player cradled his instrument and began to strum softly. There was conversation in the room a low murmuring of sound, but Isolde ate quietly, aware that she was being watched.

In answer to a question Mark had asked, Tristin was talking about the man who had been killed during their fight with the beast. Isolde, who hadn't know a man had been killed, looked over at him, startled. For just a moment their eyes met. A current, like a bolt of lightening, went all through her body and she knew she was flushing. She picked up her napkin and dabbed her mouth.

The supper dishes were being carried away when Mark clapped his hands for attention. Instantly the room was quiet.

"Tomorrow, if the new queen feels rested and ready, we will have wedding celebrations," he said. "You have all heard the story, of how Tristin killed the fire-breathing creature which plagued the riverside and seaside villages in Leinster. So one of our tournaments tomorrow will be in Tristin's honor for accomplishing the feat which brought about this marriage. Afterwards, we will have dancing."

There was polite, pleased murmuring in the room. The king rose to his feet, and gestured for Isolde to rise as well. He offered her his arm, and led her from the room. He gestured for Brangwain to follow them.

Once in the corridor, he said to Brangwain, "I have dismissed the queen's other attendants. I think the queen would be most comfortable having you alone to prepare her for the night."

Mark looked at Isolde for confirmation. She nodded to him gratefully.

"This way," Mark said, and led them through a corridor to the tower leading to their private apartments. On the threshold of Isolde's own rooms, he said, "I shall return shortly." To Brangwain he said, "I would like for you to remain long enough to serve us wine."

"Yes, your majesty," said Brangwain.

Mark left them at the doorway to Isolde's rooms.

Once they were alone, inside, Brangwain whispered, "Should we prepare you for bed? I don't know."

"No, no," said Isolde. At least Isolde didn't think so. Brangwain removed the cloak Isolde had worn to the supper room and replacing it with a lighter scarf around her shoulders. Brangwain brushed Isolde's hair loose about her shoulders until it shone.

A knock came at the door. Expecting the king, Isolde said, "Enter."

The door opened and a steward came in, wearing a red tunic stitched with gold and black trousers. He carried a tray with full bottle of wine and two goblets, which he set down on a table. Also on the tray were two plates and a honey cake.

The steward bowed and left. Isolde, feeling suddenly melancholy, went to look out the window, which faced the inner courtyard.

Brangwain was filled with worry. She wanted all to go well tonight for Isolde, but how could it, with Isolde pining for Tristin? She saw the way Tristin looked at Isolde as well and it was clear he was as in love as Isolde. Casting about for a solution, she thought about the love potion. An idea hit her with the force of a thunderbolt. Tristin and Isolde had not finished off the bottle. She went into the wardrobe and where her bags had been placed and pulled out the onion-shaped bottle and pulled out the cork. There was not enough left in the bottle for two full glasses, but there was enough for one.

Her first thought, since she no longer had the letter from the Queen of Leinster explaining to King Mark what was in the bottle, was that she should divide what was left between Isolde and Mark. But she didn't think that would be enough to work properly. Her next thought was she should give the wine to Isolde and have her fall in love with Mark.

But, she wondered, would that work? Isolde already drank the potion with Tristin. Could the potion make the same woman fall in love with two different men? Brangwain doubted it. Besides, she sensed that the potion would not work where a person's heart was turned against someone, as Isolde's was turned against Mark because of her love for Tristin.

Only one possibility remained: Give the wine to King Mark. If he fell deeply enough in love with Isolde, perhaps he'd be more likely to forgive and overlook her folly with Tristin, should he ever learn of it.

She heard footsteps approaching. She had no more time to think about what she was doing, so she quickly emptied the contents of the onion-shaped jug into one of the goblets, and poured wine from the bottle the steward had brought into the other goblet. That done, she put the onion-shaped bottle back into the leather pouch in the wardrobe.

When Mark entered Isolde's antechamber he saw, on a round table, two goblets of wine. Two cushioned chairs were positioned on either side of the table facing the fireplace.

Mark sat in one of the chairs. Soon after, Isolde entered from the bedchamber and said in the other chair. They lifted their goblets at the same time.

The taste of the wine shocked Mark. This was not the wine he had sent in. "What on earth is this?"

Brangwain and Isolde both looked at him, alarmed.

"This is not the wine my steward brought. Is it?"

Brangwain went pale. Isolde appeared bewildered. Mark reached for Isolde's goblet and smelled the liquid in her glass. Hers was regular wine.

"What have you given me?" he demanded of Brangwain.

"Wine, my lord," Brangwain said in a tight voice. "From Leinster."

Mark could only think this girl – and perhaps Isolde as well – sought to poison him. He felt deep fury. "You gave Isolde something different," he said. "Why is that?"

"*Why*, your majesty?" Brangwain was trembling now with fright.

He handed her his goblet. "You will drink it."

"Me?" Brangwain appeared shocked.

"Drink it," he said.

She took the goblet. Oddly, she did not look fearful, as he expected. "Please let me explain," she said.

"You may explain," he said. "After you drink the wine."

With a sigh she took the goblet and took a few tentative sips.

"All of it," he said, with a calm forcefulness.

She lifted the goblet and drank deeply. When she finished, she looked at Mark.

Then something astonishing happened. A soft, sweet, languid expression came over her. She looked deeply into his eyes, and smiled.

"Brangwain—?" said Isolde. Then, "Oh, no, Brangwain! What have you done?"

Brangwain smiled at Isolde. "I told you have married a magnificent man. So handsome. So strong. The perfect king." To Mark she said, "One day I hope my mistress the Princess Isolde comes to fully appreciate you."

Now Mark was the one befuddled. To Isolde, he said, "What is going on?"

"I believe," said Isolde, faltering, "I believe she tried to give you a love potion."

"A—what?"

"My mother sent it to you, as a gift, with a letter. You and I were supposed to drink it together tonight so we would fall deeply in love. But, well—"

"There was not enough for two," said Brangwain, "because—"

"You felt the need," Mark said to Brangwain, gravely astonished, "to manipulate my emotions?"

Isolde sighed deeply. "She meant well."

Brangwain was staring dreamily at Mark.

"My lord," said Isolde. "Perhaps you should excuse us for just a few minutes. I think I should talk to Brangwain in private. After we have talked, I will send her to her own bedchamber and come to your rooms shortly."

Mark was so amazed at what had just occurred he couldn't think of what to do other than agree.

When Mark left the antechamber, Isolde turned to Brangwain and said, "That was foolish! He thought you were trying to poison him!"

"I would *never* poison him," Brangwain whispered. "Isolde, I must tell that you are a fool to prefer Tristin to him. Can you not see how magnificent he is?"

"Hush! What if he hears you talking about Tristin that way!"

Isolde had doubted that the love potion was real, but now, seeing Brangwain's reaction she wondered if the Rath Luirc witch was more powerful then she had supposed. On the other hand, from the moment they'd arrived, Brangwain had been insisting that Mark was magnificent.

"Isolde, I thought to give him the potion so he'd fall so deeply in love with you that he would not realize you are no longer a virgin. Now what will you do? When he discovers you are not a virgin, he will figure out what happened on the ship. He will wonder why there was only enough love potion left for him."

"Maybe he won't know I'm not a virgin."

"He'll know."

They were silent. Then Brangwain said, "There is only one solution. I will go to him tonight instead of you."

"*What*?"

"You and I are the same size. In the darkness he will never know."

"What if he figures it out?"

"He won't. You must go in there first and get him to drink a few glasses of wine. Talk to him. Be sweet and loving. Get him to keep drinking. Then tell him you will come back here to change into your night clothing. Ask him to turn all the lights out so the room is in pitch darkness. Then I will go in your place."

"It won't work," said Isolde.

"It *will* work!"

"But," said Isolde, thrown off balance by what seemed to be a hare-brained idea. "What of *your* virginity? If you lay now with the king, your own husband will know that you are not a virgin when you marry. What will you tell him?"

"I'll make something up. I'll tell him I was raped by one of the sailors! I am not a royal princess and he is not a king. It won't matter!"

Part of Brangwain's motive, Isolde knew, was to lay with the king, who she'd obviously fallen in love with. But whatever her motives, if the ploy worked and prevented Mark from finding out that Tristin had already taken her maidenhood, it might save her and Tristin – and Mark – a lot of grief.

"Fine," Isolde said. "We will try this idea." She was frightened, though. She could see that while Mark was thoughtful and generous, his anger could be fearsome. He had, after all, calmly ordered

Brangwain to drink what he suspected was poisoned. If he found out what she had done with Tristin on the ship, he could send her home in shame – or worse.

Isolde went to the doorway leading to the passage between her apartments and the king's. At the end of an arched narrow hallway no more than six paces from end to end was another door. She went to the king's door and knocked quietly.

"Enter," he said.

He was standing by the window. She noted that the window faced west, so there was no danger of the moon shining in the window and revealing Brangwain's identity. His room was furnished much like hers, tastefully and elegantly. The room was dominated by a large bed hung with burgundy velvet. The mere sight of the bed embarrassed her. A fire in the fireplace cackled soothingly.

"My lord, I must apologize to you for what Brangwain did."

"I was most astonished."

Suddenly fearful that Brangwain's idea would lead to worse disaster than Mark finding out tonight that she was no longer a virgin, she said "I will come back ready for bed, if that is your wish."

"Is it *your* wish, Isolde?"

She was utterly startled by the question. He was asking her wish? This was her wedding night and he was her husband. Thus far in arranging this marriage nobody, had asked her wishes at all.

Instinctively she gave the correct answer. "My wish is to please you, my lord."

"I am sure you will please me, Isolde. How can you not? You are so beautiful and as graceful as an angel. The question is whether I shall please you. I can only promise you that I will try."

Something tugged in her, something like guilt and shame.

She lifted her chin and looked him directly in the face. "Shall we start all over? Shall we try again to have some wine?"

He smiled. "Certainly." He went to the next room and came back with two goblets and a bottle of wine. At the foot of the bed was a cushioned bench. He sat on the bench and invited her to sit with him.

For several minutes, they drank their wine in silence. He seemed to be watching her closely. He had such a steady gaze.

"My lovely Isolde, and you *are* lovely you know, I do hope our marriage turns out well."

Was it her own guilt, or did she hear something like a warning in his voice? "Oh, my lord, I hope so, too!" In that moment, she sincerely meant what she said.

He finished his wine and said, "Well then, Isolde. Shall we prepare for bed?"

"Perhaps we might have a little more wine first," she said. "I am feeling rather frightened."

That was true enough, but not for quite the reasons he probably thought.

He poured them both more wine. She already felt lightheaded, so she took small sips, hoping he would finish his entire goblet.

In a corner of the room was a polished table with a chess set. The pieces had been left mid-game. He must have seen her looking at the chessboard because he said, "Do you play?"

"I have learned. I can see you play."

"Yes, I play often, with my nephew Tristin."

She looked at him. She had the sense he'd mentioned Tristin's name on purpose, to test her reaction. She smiled and said, "I imagine that you win."

He smiled also. "You are an astute judge of character. In fact, I do win. Tristin is too impulsive and too impatient. When he matures he will be a fine chess player."

She watched as he took another drink. He seemed to sense that she was waiting for him to finish his wine because he emptied his goblet and set it on a nearby table. She was afraid if she drank any more, she'd swoon. He didn't seem to mind that she was not finishing hers.

She stood up and said, "I will return soon." She looked at the night candle burning on the bedside table. "Will you darken the room for me? Please?"

"Certainly," he said.

Isolde returned to her own rooms and found Brangwain dressed for bed in Isolde's own night shift and dressing gown. "Do not be too passionate with him," Isolde said.

Brangwain smiled. "Are you jealous?"

"No," Isolde said. Then she wondered if she was.

"I will play the part perfectly," said Brangwain. "You are not the only girl in this room who can enact a part." She smiled once more and said, "This is my night to be a royal princess."

Brangwain blew out the night candles in Isolde's room. Then, in pitch darkness, she crept from the room.

Isolde intended to wait until Brangwain returned, but once she put her head on her pillow, the darkness combined with the wine combined with the events of a long day caused her to drift into a heavy sleep.

Sometime later, and she didn't know how long, she awoke to Brangwain tugging on her arm. "Wake up, wake up," Brangwain whispered fiercely.

Isolde stretched languidly. Then she remembered. She bolted awake.

"Did you fool him?"

"Easily. But only because he is in love with you."

Isolde sighed with relief that the thing was done.

"I stand by what I said before, and I mean it even more now. Tristin is nothing compared to him. Perhaps Tristin knows how to fight, but off the battlefield, he bends like a reed. Tristin probably didn't want to rule the Duchy of Brittany because he knows he isn't that kind of man. But Mark is truly a *king*!"

The next day, as King Mark promised his court and nobles, there was reveling and dancing and jousting to celebrate his wedding to Isolde. For the jousting, Isolde sat high in the stands under the royal canopy next to Mark. The trumpets, the fanfare, the banners, the cheering were familiar to Isolde. She supposed tournaments were the same everywhere. Tristin was easily the strongest knight in the contests. When the contests were over, the knights changed from their armor into court clothing. There was dancing in the great hall. Isolde led two of the dances with Mark, but otherwise, she was content to sit and watch. She and Tristin carefully avoided each other.

Late in the afternoon, the king had official business, so Isolde retired to her own rooms. She was standing at the window of her bedchamber looking into the inner courtyard when Brangwain entered.

Isolde took one look at Brangwain and knew something was wrong. "What?" she demanded. "Tell me."

Brangwain sat on the bed. Isolde sat next to her. "Tell me," Isolde said again.

"Brace yourself. I wanted to make sure you heard it from me instead of someone else so your reaction does not give you away."

"Please tell me," said Isolde, feeling panic. "Now!"

"Tristin has asked permission to leave the court. He has told the king he wants to return to his native Brittany to find a wife."

Isolde felt as if ice had been poured down her back. "I see," she said.

"It was smart of him," Brangwain said. "If he doesn't leave, and stay away for a very long time, one of you will give yourselves away."

"Yes," Isolde said. "I suppose so."

"He has asked me to give you a message. I considered not giving you the message, for your own good."

"You must tell me!"

"He wants you to meet him tonight, when the moon rises, so he can tell you goodbye. There is a walled orchard in the courtyard. He says he will meet you there."

Isolde stood up and went back to the window.

"Don't go," said Brangwain. "Please don't be foolish. Don't risk everything for a silly goodbye."

Isolde did not answer.

"But your majesty," said Lord Godwin, "I have heard the reports from the crew that sailed with Tristin."

King Mark and Lord Godwin were in the throne room. All the other members of the king's council had been dismissed. Lord Godwin had remained, insisting he had secret intelligence for the king's ears alone.

"You will say no more." Mark spoke quietly, but firmly.

"Yes, your majesty." Lord Godwin bowed. Once dismissed, he turned and walked from the hall.

Waiting just outside and around a corner was Lord Denoalan. "Well?" Denoalan asked.

"He won't listen or believe. Tomorrow Tristin leaves. We will keep careful watch tonight."

Isolde knew better than to meet Tristin at moonrise in the courtyard. Brangwain was right. It was foolish to risk everything just to say goodbye.

Nonetheless, late that night she stood fully dressed in her bedchamber, watching out the window. When the moon showed over the horizon, she pulled on a woolen cloak lined with fur and crept quietly from her room into the corridor, which was dark except for a single torch mounted high on the wall. The door leading to the courtyard and walled orchard was directly downstairs. She hurried down the stairs, which were much wider and less steep then the stairs in the Castle of Leinster, and not as cold.

Her leather-soled slippers tapped lightly against the stone stairs. Once she reached the bottom, she pushed open the heavy door and slipped out into the cold night.

Both Denoalan and Godfrey, hidden in an alcove of the stair tower, watched Isolde hurry down the stairs.

"When his majesty learns the truth," Godfrey whispered, "Do you think he will destroy her? Or just Tristin?"

"It doesn't matter much to me," said Denoalan. "All I care about is that the time has finally come for his majesty to see just what kind of stuff his beloved nephew is made of. If we are not careful, he may be our king one day."

The two nobles walked up the stairs to the king's chambers and knocked urgently.

Geoff, the king's trusted steward, answered the door. "What is happening?"

"Tell his majesty that the queen has been kidnapped," said Godwin.

"*Kidnapped?*"

King Mark appeared behind Geoff, pulling on his dressing gown.

"What on God's earth is going on?" Mark demanded.

"It appears the queen has been kidnapped," said Godwin. "We heard the commotion. I believe you will find she is not in her bedchamber."

Mark gave Godwin a look of cold amazement. He turned and strode back into his private bedchamber, then out the door to the private passageway leading to Isolde's rooms. He opened the door to her bedroom and saw that indeed, she was not there.

He took the night candle and looked in each of her rooms. Quietly he pushed open the door to the maid's room. Inside, Brangwain was sound asleep. Otherwise, the chambers were empty.

He did not think for a moment that Isolde had been kidnapped. He knew – as did Godwin and Denoalan – that Tristin and Isolde were together somewhere. He felt deep anger that they would humiliate him this way.

He returned to his own rooms. Godwin and Denoalan were waiting in his antechamber. "We must find her," said Godwin.

Mark was trapped. He had no wish to catch his nephew and wife in a heated embrace. On the other hand, he could think of no excuse for telling his noblemen that he refused to investigate.

"Very well," said Mark.

"They are most likely in the courtyard," said Godwin.

"If I stay here," said Tristin, "I know what would happen. I'd never be able to resist you." His arms were around her. She put her head on his shoulder.

"I understand," she said. She had tears in her eyes.

Just then, Tristin looked up at the castle and said, "God's nails!"

"What?" Isolde cried.

"There are shadows in the windows," he whispered urgently. "Someone is coming!"

"Coming? Are you sure?"

"Yes!"

She looked at Tristin's face and saw that he was almost stricken with fear. "What shall we do?" she cried.

Instantly, they fell away from each other.

"Come," Tristin whispered. "Sit here, on the bench. We will talk loudly enough, and innocently enough, so that anyone may hear us."

Yes, he was right. They must talk! But about what?

Isolde heard a rustling sound and knew someone was on the other side of the wall. She drew in a deep breath to steady herself. In a clear voice, she said, "Thank you for coming to tell me goodbye. If we said goodbye in front of everyone, how suspicious people would be! But the knight who ridded my father's kingdom of a fire-breathing dragon shall always have my friendship."

"And I shall treasure your friendship," said Tristin.

"There was something else I wanted to talk to you about," Isolde said. She realized she was chattering nervously, but what else could she do? "I wanted to talk to you about the disaster with the love potion."

"What disaster?"

"Brangwain drank the love potion and has fallen in love with my husband! It is so embarrassing the way she swoons over him."

Tristin, caught by surprise, laughed. "You jest!"

"I do not. She is completely in love with him."

"Are you jealous?" Tristin asked, understanding his cue.

"Perhaps I am."

"Well, then. I think you should send her back to Leinster before she steals your husband away from you."

"I think perhaps I should."

"Your jealousy over Brangwain is nothing next to the problems I face with Lords Denoalan and Godfrey." Tristin turned slightly, aware that his uncle may be the person standing on the other side of the wall. "They are always looking to twist any innocent thing I do to make me look bad."

Isolde, who had no idea who Denoalan and Godwin were, went along. "That's just too bad."

"They are so terrified I may one day be their king, they plot against me at every turn."

"Now, I must go in," she said. "This would look completely wrong if someone saw us."

She stood up. Tristin stood up, too. Very softly, so that nobody on the other side of the wall could hear, he whispered, "I will love you always, Isolde."

"And I you," she whispered so quietly she made almost no sound. "But Tristin, you must never come back." She meant what she said. She loved Tristin, of course, and couldn't bear to lose him. But now, so close to being caught, she was equally terrified at the thought of being shamed forever.

Using his normal voice, Tristin said, "I know you will be very happy with my uncle."

"I know it, too," she said, loudly and clearly.

Listening, Mark felt intense relief. Once Isolde ran from the courtyard back into the stair tower, he himself turned and walked back to the castle.

Godwin and Denoalan followed him into the stair tower.

Once they were inside, he faced Godwin and Denoalan, and said, "I heard nothing that could be called treason."

"But, your majesty," Godwin said. "Your nephew lured her from her bedchamber in the dead of night—"

"It was ill-advised for them to meet in the dead of night. It was ill-advised and foolish. But it was not treason. I am growing tired of you two making so much trouble. Good night."

He climbed the stairs and entered his own chambers and warmed himself by the fire. He waited long enough for Isolde to be warmed as well, and settled into her own bed. Then he went to her door, knocked softly to give warning, and entered her bedchamber. A night candle burned by her beside. Her glorious hair was spread over the pillow, glowing in the candlelight. He sat on her bed, and touched her shoulder. She stretched languidly, like a cat, and opened her eyes.

Seeing him, she smiled.